WARRIORS OF HISTORY

AZTEC WARRIORS

by Mary Englar

Consultant:
Dr. Colin M. Maclachlan
John Christy Barr Distinguished Professor of History
Tulane University
New Orleans, Louisiana

Capstone
press

Mankato, Minnesota

Edge Books are published by Capstone Press,
151 Good Counsel Drive, P.O. Box 669, Mankato, Minnesota 56002.
www.capstonepress.com

Library of Congress Cataloging-in-Publication Data
Englar, Mary.
     Aztec warriors / by Mary Englar.
     p. cm. — (Edge books. Warriors of history)
     Includes bibliographical references and index.
     ISBN-13: 978-1-4296-1309-5 (hardcover)
     ISBN-10: 1-4296-1309-2 (hardcover)
     1. Aztecs — Wars. 2. Indian weapons — Mexico. 3. Aztecs — History.
4. Aztecs — Government relations. I. Title.
F1219.76.W37E64 2008
972'.018 — dc22   2007029956

Summary: Describes the life of an Aztec warrior, including his training, weapons, and
     what led to the downfall of his society.

Editorial Credits
Mandy Robbins, editor; Thomas Emery, set designer; Kyle Grenz, book designer;
     Jo Miller, photo researcher; Tod Smith, illustrator; Krista Ward, colorist

Photo Credits
Alamy/North Wind Picture Archives, 4
Art Resource, N.Y./British Museum, 16–17; Schalkwijk, 8–9
Corbis/Danny Lehman, 15; Kevin Fleming, cover
Getty Images Inc./Bridgemen Art Library/Baron von Friedrich Alexander Humboldt, 6;
     Rischgitz, 10
The Granger Collection, New York, 7
Mary Evans Picture Library, 20
SuperStock, Inc., 13, 23; Jack Novak, 24; Steve Vidler, 28–29; Stock Montage, 27

1 2 3 4 5 6 13 12 11 10 09 08

TABLE OF CONTENTS

CHAPTER I
The Valley of Mexico..................................... 4

CHAPTER II
Fierce Warriors.. 10

CHAPTER III
The Weapons of War 16

CHAPTER IV
The End of an Empire 24

FEATURES

Aztec Warrior diagram............................... 18

Glossary 30

Read More 31

Internet Sites... 31

Index.. 32

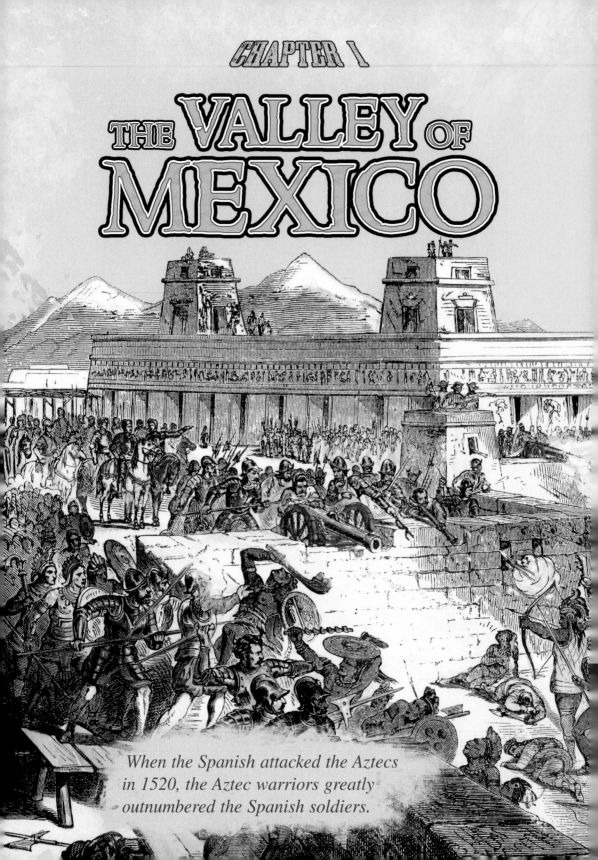

CHAPTER 1

THE VALLEY OF MEXICO

When the Spanish attacked the Aztecs in 1520, the Aztec warriors greatly outnumbered the Spanish soldiers.

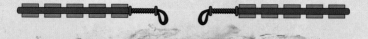

LEARN ABOUT:

- Defending their cities
- The empire in the valley
- Great warriors

At dawn, drums sounded the Spanish attack on Tenochtitlan. Thousands of Aztec warriors raced toward about 500 Spanish soldiers. The emperor and his best Aztec warriors led the charge. They carried sharp swords made of black stone and colorful feathered shields. The warriors screamed the names of their cities as they ran.

Aztec archers shot hundreds of arrows. Slingers aimed stones. Warriors used dart-throwers to launch sharp darts. The darts pierced the soldiers' armor, causing deep, bloody wounds. Under heavy attack, the Spanish fell back. They pulled on their horses' reins to keep steady.

The Aztecs did not have an alphabet. They used pictures to represent names, places, dates, and numbers.

EDGE FACT

Aztec writers recorded history in books called codices. Much of what we know about the Aztecs comes from these books.

Aztec warriors wore very little armor compared to Spanish soldiers.

The Aztecs continued to charge at their enemies. Some warriors peered out between the animal teeth on their helmets. They chopped and sliced with swords. Others jabbed with spears. The Aztec warriors fought fiercely to protect their great city.

THE AZTEC EMPIRE

Around 1250, the Mexica Indians entered the Valley
of Mexico from the north. The Mexica claimed a rocky
island in the middle of Lake Texcoco. There, they built
Tenochtitlan. In 1428, the city-states of Tenochtitlan,
Texcoco, and Tlacopan worked together to rule the valley.
Together the people were called the Aztecs.

*The Mexica Indians began building
the city of Tenochtitlan in 1325.*

The Aztecs conquered every city in the valley.
Each city had to pay the Aztecs in weapons,
food, valuable feathers, and jewelry. The Aztecs
were constantly at war. They became the greatest
warriors in Central America.

CHAPTER II
FIERCE WARRIORS

Aztec warriors fought each other to improve their fighting skills.

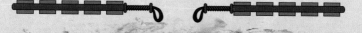

LEARN ABOUT:
- *A warrior society*
- *Aztec education*
- *Jaguar and Eagle warriors*

All Aztec boys trained for war. The best fighters entered military societies. Successful warriors were honored by the emperor at yearly festivals. Most warriors came from the noble classes. These were the wealthy families who ran the government and owned land.

The nobles also chose new emperors from the best warriors. Aztec emperors had to be brave warriors. The Aztec Empire depended on military strength to gain new land and increase its wealth. If the emperors were weak, the empire would not grow.

All men, both farmers and trained warriors, had to fight when the emperor called them to war. Even a poor young man could become a respected warrior if he fought bravely in battle. War was a way for common people to gain wealth and land.

AZTEC SCHOOLS

Aztec boys and girls were raised differently. Some girls went to school, but most were trained at home to cook, sew, and care for children. Aztec boys went to school between the ages of 6 and 13.

The sons of emperors and nobles went to special schools. They started school at age 5. The boys lived at the schools until they were old enough to go to war. Schools prepared Aztec boys for life as priests, leaders, or warriors. The boys studied history, arithmetic, astronomy, and warfare. Experienced warriors taught the boys how to use Aztec weapons.

GAINING EXPERIENCE

When war broke out, experienced warriors took young men with them. Beginning at age 15, the youths carried supplies and weapons for the warriors. At age 20, some young men chose to become warriors. At their first battle, the young warriors tried to capture enemies. If they captured enemies without help, they proved their bravery. If they never took a captive, the older warriors shaved the young men's heads to shame them.

Aztec warriors attacked with wooden clubs called maquahuitl, meaning "war clubs."

RULES OF WAR

Aztec men learned to obey their war leaders' orders. If a warrior attacked before the leader's order, he was killed. If he fled the battlefield before the order to retreat, he was also killed. Aztec warriors learned during childhood that bravery and self-control in war brought them respect, wealth, and success.

MILITARY SOCIETIES

Warriors had to prove their bravery in battle before they could enter a military society. The society warriors lived in a section of the emperor's palace. Each time a warrior took prisoners, he earned a higher rank. Enemy prisoners were sacrificed after the battles to thank the Aztec gods.

Two of the societies were the Eagle and Jaguar warriors. These warriors wore suits made of animal skins or cloth covered with feathers. Jaguar warriors wore complete suits of feathered cloth that looked like jaguar fur. As the warriors took more prisoners, they earned the right to wear the most beautiful war suits and helmets.

This statue shows the uniform of
an Eagle warrior. It is displayed at the
Museum of the Temple Mayor in Mexico.

CHAPTER III
THE
WEAPONS
OF WAR

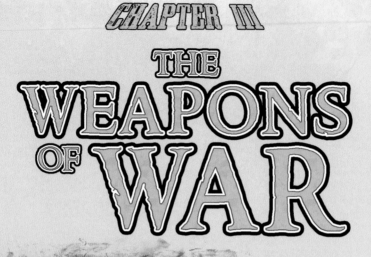

LEARN ABOUT:
- *Bows, arrows, and slings*
- *Spears and swords*
- *Aztec armor*

The Aztecs used ceremonial knives to sacrifice prisoners of war to their gods.

Aztec men did not carry weapons during peacetime. Each city stored weapons in armories. Men went to the armory to get weapons when they were called to war.

Aztec warriors carried bows or slings, which they also used for hunting. The bows were about 5 feet (1.5 meters) long. The arrows were tipped with volcanic rock, stone, or fishbone. Weapon makers made each arrow the same size to increase accuracy. The best archers could shoot two or three arrows at once.

Aztec slings were made from woven fibers. Warriors used the slings to hurl stones at enemies. The round stones were hand-shaped to all be the same size. The Spanish wrote that the stones were as dangerous as arrows to their armies. It was impossible to avoid so many stones fired at the same time.

Headdress
Aztec chiefs often had layers of gold in their military headdress.

Shield
Aztec shields could be strapped to the warrior's forearm so both his hands were free.

Spear
The point of an Aztec spear was lined with sharp jagged stones.

Military society warriors shot sharp darts as they got close to the enemy. Darts were tipped with obsidian stone, fishbone, or copper. Warriors used dart-throwers that were carved from wood. At one end, a hook held the dart in place when the warrior swung his arm. The darts flew faster than arrows.

HAND-TO-HAND COMBAT

The emperor and military society warriors led attacks. They carried swords and spears. The swords were about 3 feet (1 meter) long and 3 to 4 inches (7 to 10 centimeters) wide. Along the sides, the Aztecs glued pieces of obsidian stone. The swords were sharp enough to kill with one blow.

The Aztecs used spears for thrusting and slashing. Spears were about 6 feet (2 meters) long. The Aztecs also used these sharp spears to shave their heads.

*The Aztecs sacrificed prisoners
to honor their gods.*

BLOODY BATTLES

Aztec battles were very bloody. Swords could cut off an enemy's head. Darts punched holes in armor.

Aztecs usually faced much smaller armies. The screams of thousands of Aztec warriors frightened even the experienced Spanish soldiers. Enemies of the Aztecs fought hard. If they were captured alive, they knew they would be sacrificed to the Aztec gods.

HUMAN SACRIFICE

Before the 1600s, many people living in Mexico sacrificed humans to their gods. The Aztecs took their prisoners to the top of the main temple. There, priests laid the prisoner on his back on a large stone. The priests cut the prisoner's beating heart out of his chest. They offered it to their most important god.

The Aztecs believed the gods used their own blood to make man. For the Aztecs, blood was the most important gift they could offer the gods.

When the main temple in Tenochtitlan was completed, the emperor ordered the sacrifice of thousands of prisoners. It is estimated that between 20,000 and 80,000 prisoners were killed.

BATTLE DRESS

Most Aztec warriors wore no armor. Archers and slingers stayed behind the front lines and never fought hand to hand. The military society warriors wore cotton armor and wood or bone helmets. They carried shields made of bamboo, wood, or copper.

Armor was made of cotton sewn between two pieces of cloth. It covered the body, but not the arms or legs. Over the armor, warriors wore their war suits. The war suits covered the whole body, including the arms and legs.

Helmets were made of animal heads stretched over wood. Jaguar, eagle, wolf, or mountain lion jaws framed the warriors' faces.

EDGE FACT

The Aztecs' huge armies frightened their enemies. The Aztecs used 200,000 warriors to capture some cities.

Aztec warriors traveled in small boats through water-filled passages called canals.

CHAPTER IV

THE END OF AN EMPIRE

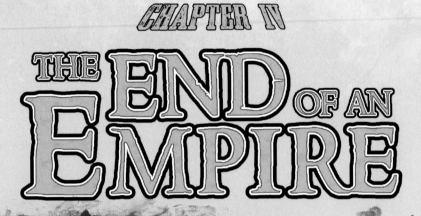

LEARN ABOUT:

- *Cortés' invasion*
- *Emperor Montezuma*
- *Destroying Tenochtitlan*

When the Aztecs first met Cortés, they may have thought he was a god.

As the Aztec Empire grew, Tenochtitlan did not have enough food to feed its 200,000 people. People from conquered cities in the valley had to send more goods to the Aztec emperor to feed the people of Tenochtitlan. If they refused, the Aztec army destroyed their cities and sacrificed the citizens to their gods. Many local people feared and hated the Aztecs.

In 1519, Spanish explorer Hernán Cortés sailed to the coast of Mexico in search of gold. Cortés had heard of a great empire of gold in the Valley of Mexico. Cortés brought 500 soldiers with him to Mexico. He hoped to conquer the Aztecs and take the gold he thought they had. Thousands of local Indians joined Cortés to help him defeat the Aztecs.

When Cortés and his men first saw the Valley of Mexico and its cities, they were amazed. Tenochtitlan was built on islands in Lake Texcoco. White stone temples shone in the bright sun. Long bridges crossed the lake to connect the city to the land.

In November 1519, Emperor Montezuma invited Cortés and his men into Tenochtitlan. No one knows why Montezuma did not fight the Spanish at first. Some experts think he didn't know if the Spanish wanted to fight or befriend the Aztecs. Others believe Montezuma thought Cortés was a god.

Within a week, the Spanish arrested Montezuma. Still, Montezuma did not order his people to attack the Spanish. The Aztecs finally rebelled in July 1520. They chased the Spanish out of the city, but Montezuma was killed. No one knows if the Spanish or the Aztecs killed him. The new Aztec emperor, Cuautemoc, called for war.

EDGE FACT
Montezuma is the Spanish spelling for the emperor's name. Historians think Moteuczomah or Moctezuma is a more accurate pronunciation.

Montezuma became the
Aztec emperor in 1502.

Cortés planned his final attack well. He knew he could not fight the Aztecs on the narrow causeways that crossed the lake. Instead, he surrounded Tenochtitlan in May 1521. He cut off the Aztecs' food supplies and fresh water. Still, the Aztecs kept the Spanish out of Tenochtitlan for three months.

When the Spanish entered Tenochtitlan in August, they found a dying city. Disease had killed half of the people, and the rest were starving. The last few warriors fought bravely until their emperor was captured. The Aztecs surrendered to Cortés on August 13, 1521. It had taken the Spanish less than two years to destroy the Aztec Empire.

Once Cortés took Tenochtitlan, he ordered his men to destroy the city. On top of the ruins, he built a new Spanish capital. He named the city Mexico City after the Mexica indians who had lived there. The Mexica Indian name was also later used for the valley and eventually for the country of Mexico.

Today, construction workers in Mexico City often discover pieces of Tenochtitlan. Digging beneath the streets, historians are still learning about the history of the Aztecs.

The remains of Aztec pyramids stand in front of the Spanish Church of Santiago in Mexico City.

GLOSSARY

armory (AR-muh-ree) — a place where weapons are stored

empire (EM-pire) — a large area of land ruled by one government or king

noble (NOH-buhl) — a wealthy, upper-class person of high rank

obsidian (uhb-SI-dee-uhn) — glass formed by cooling lava

sacrifice (SAK-ruh-fisse) — to kill an animal or person in order to honor a god

Tenochtitlan (te-nawch-tee-TLAHN) — the capital of the Aztec Empire

READ MORE

Lourie, Peter. *Hidden World of the Aztec.* Honesdale, Penn.: Boyds Mills Press, 2006.

Macdonald, Fiona. *How to Be an Aztec Warrior.* How to Be Series. Washington, D.C.: National Geographic, 2005.

Smalley, Roger. *The Aztecs: the Rise and Fall of a Great Empire.* Mankato, Minn.: Red Brick Learning, 2004.

INTERNET SITES

FactHound offers a safe, fun way to find Internet sites related to this book. All of the sites on FactHound have been researched by our staff.

Here's how:
1. Visit *www.facthound.com*
2. Choose your grade level.
3. Type in this book ID **1429613092** for age-appropriate sites. You may also browse subjects by clicking on letters, or by clicking on pictures and words.
4. Click on the **Fetch It** button.

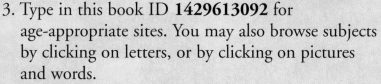

FactHound will fetch the best sites for you!

INDEX

armor, 5, 7, 20, 22

armories, 17

attacks, 5, 13, 19, 28

Aztec Empire, 11, 25, 28

Aztec gods, 14, 16, 20, 21, 25, 26

ceremonial knives, 16

codices, 6

Cortés, Hernán, 24, 25–26, 28–29

emperors, 5, 11, 12, 14, 19, 21, 25, 28
Cuautemoc, 26
Montezuma, 26, 27

Lake Texcoco, 8, 26

Mexica Indians, 8, 9, 29

Mexico City, 29

military societies, 11, 14, 19, 22
Eagle warriors, 14, 15
Jaguar warriors, 14

prisoners, 14, 16, 20, 21

sacrifices, 14, 16, 20, 21, 25

schools, 12

Spanish, 4, 5, 7, 17, 20, 25, 26, 28–29

Tenochtitlan, 5, 8, 9, 21, 25, 26, 28–29

Texcoco, 8, 26

Tlacopan, 8

war, 9, 11, 12, 13, 17, 26

weapons, 9, 12, 17, 20
bows and arrows, 5, 17
clubs, 13
darts, 5, 19, 20
helmets, 7, 14, 22
shields, 5, 22
slings, 5, 17
spears, 7, 19
swords, 5, 7, 19, 20

Valley of Mexico, 8–9, 25, 26, 29

wounds, 5, 20